Martin MacGregor's Snowman

Lisa Broadie Cook

Illustrations by Adam McCauley

Walker & Company
New York

It was November. All Martin MacGregor wanted to do was build a snowman. But so far this season, no snow had come.

"I live for snowman building," said Martin MacGregor. "Last year, I built the biggest snowman in the neighborhood."

Martin tried making a snowman using the marshmallows in his hot chocolate. But the marshmallow snowman melted too quickly and ended up as little more than a marshmallow mustache.

"Even the birds look like they want some snow," he grumbled.

His mom was going to the basement with the laundry. "Be glad we don't have to shovel the driveway. Keep an eye on your sister for a minute."

Martin MacGregor sighed.

His mother didn't understand.

He glanced at his sister in the high chair. She didn't understand either. But as she ate her pancakes, Martin got a fabulous idea.

He took out a brand-new bag of flour, and dumped it—*whoosh!*—over his syrupy sister.

"A snow baby!" yelled Martin triumphantly.

"WAAAH!" yelled his sister.

"MARTIN!" yelled his mother.

Martin MacGregor waited for the snow in his cooling-off chair.

In December, there was still no snow. Not even for a white Christmas. One day a light dusting barely covered the grass, but Martin MacGregor was excited anyway. He called to his dad, "If you need me, I'll be snowman building, building, building."

Martin MacGregor piled and piled and piled the snow. Martin was disgusted. "It won't stick together!" he yelled.

His dad was backing his car out of the garage. "Well, I for one am glad the roads won't be slick. Don't forget to take Sadie for a walk while I'm out."

Martin MacGregor rolled his eyes. His father didn't understand. He glanced at Sadie with the leash in her mouth. Sadie didn't understand either. But as Sadie wagged her tail, Martin got an amazing idea.

Sadie sat calmly as Martin MacGregor glued cotton balls all over her fur. But when Martin's dad returned home, Sadie tore off running. Bits of cotton covered the yard.

"Presenting . . . Sadie the snow dog!" yelled Martin.

"WOOF!" barked Sadie.

"MARTIN!" yelled his dad.

Martin MacGregor waited for the snow while he gave Sadie a bath.

In January, the weather was cloudy, gray, and gloomy. But there was no snow.

Martin thought his mashed potatoes had possibilities, but they made little more than a mushy mess. Martin sighed and plopped his head down on the table.

His mom said, "Go take your bath, Martin. Maybe that will cheer you up. And please be finished before the ladies from my book club arrive."

Martin MacGregor poured in the entire bottle of bubble bath and turned on the whirlpool. It made the perfect foam. As he lay there, Martin MacGregor got an incredible idea.

With the foam covering every inch of him, he stood up to admire himself in the mirror. Then he headed downstairs into the living room.

"Look everybody, a snowman!" he announced.

"Oh, Martin," said his mom.

The bubbles began to slide downward at an alarmingly quick pace.

The entire book club stared with open mouths at Martin in his nothingness.

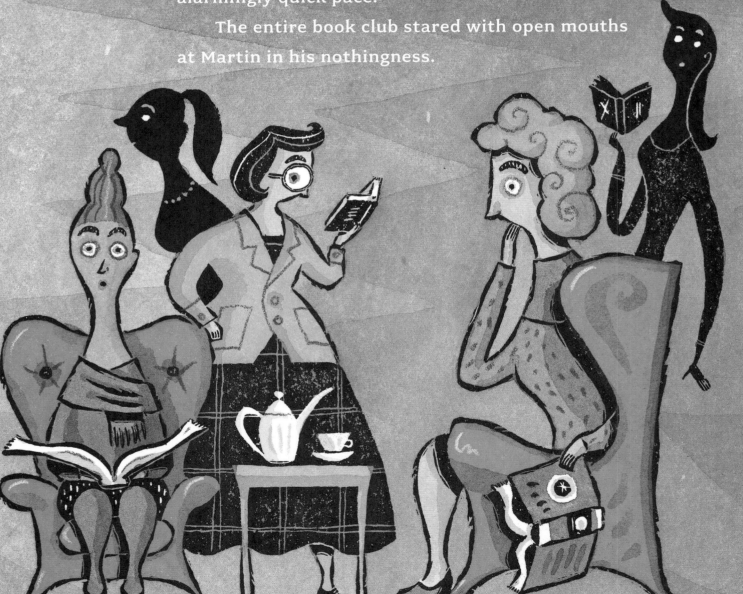

Martin MacGregor waited for the snow
in his room with the lights out.

In February, the weatherman finally predicted a huge snowstorm.

Martin leaped out of bed bright and early the next morning and sprinted to the window. But there was *NO SNOW!!!*

"Crummy weatherman," mumbled Martin MacGregor. "I'm moving to Alaska!"

"Don't forget your boots," said his dad.

That day Martin wore all white and tried stuffing his clothes to look like a snowman, but he just looked silly.

In art class, Martin MacGregor painted an enormous snowman. His art teacher, Mrs. French, exclaimed: "Martin, you have captured the true essence of a snowman."

Martin MacGregor gave her a disgusted look and yelled, "THE ESSENCE OF A SNOWMAN IS *SNOW!*" He tore up his paper and threw it on the floor.

Martin MacGregor waited for the snow
in the principal's office.

March came. It was unusually warm.

"Come on, Son," called Martin's dad, "help me with the yard work on this beautiful spring day."

Martin MacGregor tried to make a grass man out of grass clippings and leaves, but it blew away with a gust of wind.

After working in the yard, Martin got a wonderful
idea. On the front porch he used his dad's shaving cream
and his mom's lipstick to create a snowman.

"All I have is a droopy, gloopy lump of nothing,"
he said. He was not amused.

His baby sister *was* amused. She finger painted
the windows. She finger painted the door. She covered
herself in shaving cream.

When Martin's mom and dad came out on the porch,
they were *not* amused.

"I wish I had gone to Alaska," Martin whispered.

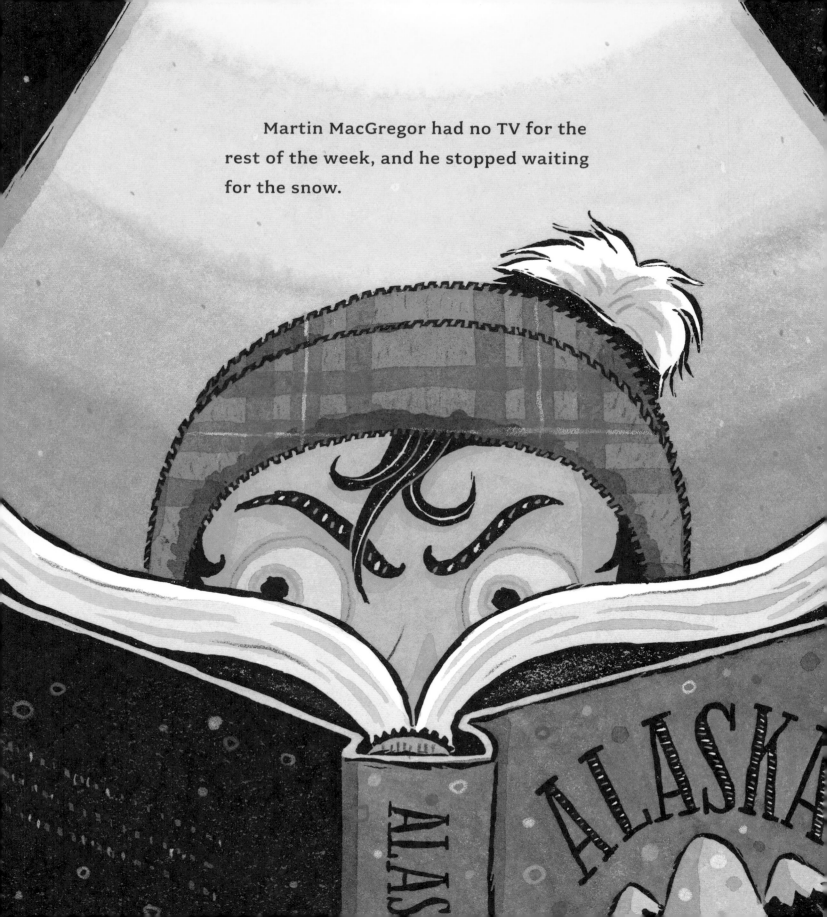

Martin MacGregor had no TV for the rest of the week, and he stopped waiting for the snow.

On the first day of April, Martin woke up with a jolt. It was brighter than usual outside. He raced to the window.

Martin MacGregor could not believe his eyes.

Everything was covered in sparkling
white snow. He stared at a frozen world.
"Awesome! A blizzard!" he cried, and he
threw on his clothes and ran out the door.

School was canceled for three whole days, and
Martin made a snowman, a snow lady, a snow boy,
a snow girl, *and* a snow baby. His mom and dad even
helped. Despite frozen ears and a frozen nose, frozen
fingers and frozen toes, he couldn't have been happier.
Martin MacGregor finally got to build his snowman.

Then came May. All Martin MacGregor wanted
to do was go swimming and build sand castles.

For Dave, Hallie, and Christian —L. B. C.

For Nicholas —A. M.

First published in the United States of America in 2003 by Walker Publishing Company, Inc.

Published simultaneously in Canada by Fitzhenry and Whiteside, Markham, Ontario L3R 4T8

For information about permission to reproduce selections from this book, write to Permissions, Walker & Company, 435 Hudson Street, New York, New York 10014

Library of Congress Cataloging-in-Publication Data
Cook, Lisa Broadie.
Martin MacGregor's snowman / Lisa Broadie Cook ; illustrations by Adam McCauley
      p. cm.
Summary: While anxiously awaiting the arrival of snow, Martin MacGregor, who built the biggest snowman in the neighborhood last year, tries to build one with substitute materials.
ISBN 0-8027-8858-0 (HC) — ISBN 0-8027-8859-9 (RE)
[1. Snowmen—Fiction. 2. Snow—Fiction.] I. McCauley, Adam, ill. II. Title.

PZ7.C76987Mar 2003
[E]—dc21

                                        2002192418

The artist used mixed media on watercolor paper to create the illustrations for this book. The text and display type were set in Fairplex.

Book design by Cynthia Wigginton

Visit Walker & Company's Web site at www.walkeryoungreaders.com

Printed in Hong Kong

10 9 8 7 6 5 4 3 2 1